Cosy Burrow Books

VALKYRIE ACADEMY DRAGON ALLIANCE
Book Four

INFLICTED

I0585547

"*Inflicted* is filled with quick-witted dragons, plenty of action, and commanding heroines." - Stefanie B., Red Adept Editing Line Editor

VALKYRIE ACADEMY DRAGON ALLIANCE BOOKS

MARKED (PREQUEL-SHORT STORY)
CHOSEN
VANISHED
SCORNED
INFLICTED
EMPOWERED
AMBUSHED
WARNED
ABDUCTED
BESIEGED
DECEIVED

Cosy Burrow Books

VALKYRIE ACADEMY DRAGON ALLIANCE

INFLICTED

KATRINA COPE

ISBN: 978-0-6486613-3-7

Colin & Glenys ~ Thank you for the peace you supplied (with a view) while writing this book

GET UPDATES & NOTIFICATIONS OF GIVEAWAYS

Would you like a FREE copy of Marked?
Visit here:
https://www.katrinacopebooks.com/valkyrie-academy-
dragon-alliance
Through this link you can sign up for my newsletter
and receive a FREE copy of Marked plus updates
about my fantasy books, sales and notification of
giveaways.

- CHAPTER ONE -

The pounding of my shoes on the floor reverberates off the walls of the corridor. My feet won't run fast enough. I must move quicker. By the time I reach the main door of the academy, my lungs are screaming for air. I glance at my left hand. The strange current that ran down my arm and out my hand before firing into Rota is a mystery to me. No reasoning in my mind can explain what happened—not even the old woman who touched me only moments before. It was my second encounter with her, and although both meetings were brief, every fiber of my being makes me think she may be a witch. She was too old to be a Valkyrie and too weird to be normal. Although I'm not an expert in this field since I haven't met a witch before.

I burst out of the front door of the academy and spin around to check if anybody is following me. Coming up empty, I keep going. Despite my panic, I can't help thinking about how strange it is that the elderly lady entered the academy. Making things weirder was the briefness of our meeting. It was almost as though she'd sought me out and followed me here.

My eyes flick, searching relentlessly. Perhaps the old lady is following me. I can't see her, but that doesn't mean she's not. I'm not even sure how she knows my mother, whom I haven't seen since starting at the academy. As a rule, all students who join the academy must break contact with their families. Academy students must become hardened warriors and learn how to cope and deal with problems by fighting their way through them.

I'll have to consult the library to see what it says about witches. Perhaps it holds more books like *The Tales of How Brynhildr Got Her Wings*. I know it's just a myth, but I have never given up hope that one day I can become like the winged Valkyries and help reap souls for Valhalla—even if I can't grow wings.

My left arm tingles with the strange sensation that continues to run through its veins, and I rub my hand up and down it. Surely it couldn't have been magic that passed through my arm. Could it? And why would it be this arm? My fingers tickle the scar, and a thought runs through my head. It is the arm that the beast marked when I scared it away from stealing Elan's egg.

I shake my head. No. I must be imagining things. I didn't do anything to Rota back in the bathroom. She must've had a medical seizure or something. I couldn't possibly have harmed her. For a start, I am wingless. That means I have no extraordinary power, and I only work for the winged Valkyries as a slave. On top of that, Valkyries can't have magic, as far as I know.

As I stare out into the open lands, I think about running to my room and talking it over with Hildr and Eir, but I'm not sure they will understand. Even if they do, I doubt they could do anything to help me. During all the time we've spent together in the last couple of years we have lived together, we have never talked about magic.

I shake my head and remind myself this isn't magic. It's just a figment of my imagination. Rota had some kind of medical seizure or something. That's got to be all.

I stop in my tracks—there is no need for me to be running. This isn't my fault. I change direction and decide to speak with Elan. After all, she has been through a lot today because of me. Her mind must be in a flurry with events from the past day, as well as trying to cope with the injury she received while defending me against the other dragon. She has only been in my life for such a short time, but I am growing more fond of her every day. These dragons are not the vicious creatures that others have led us to believe—well, at least not the dragons like Elan and her clan, who have shown us kindness. As for the other dragons, I should fear the ones in the wild and the ones the winged Valkyries have treated poorly. I do not hold their bitterness against them. If I were treated as badly as they are, I'm pretty sure I would also become vicious.

I stroll to the place where I left Elan. I instructed her to stay invisible. We don't want

Odin or anyone else capturing her again. She is meant to be free.

I don't see her, but as I wander closer to the area, a rumbling noise catches my attention. I shake my head. Her snoring would alert the deaf—it's that loud. So much for staying in hiding. The snoring crescendos as I get closer, and I follow it until I collide with her side. A strange pride fills me as I run my hands along her body against the direction of her scales. Pain shoots up my leg as something snares it. That will definitely be a bruise later. As I work my way down and grasp the object within my hands, I feel its shape. I realize it's one of her horns.

"Elan." I shake the horn. "Elan…"

A short burst of snorts interrupts the monotone rhythm of snores, followed by a clicking of the tongue, as though she is savoring the flavor of something. This pauses, then her slow and lingering snores break the silence again.

I stare at the vacant spot in disbelief then reach down to grab her horn and shake it again. "Elan!"

Slowly, her golden scales form before me, and she raises a weary eyebrow, staring at me vacantly with her golden-brown eyes. I already feel better.

Kara? Her tongue clicks against the roof of her mouth again, then she yawns, exposing her enormous mouth filled with sharp, jagged teeth. *Kara, is that you?*

"Who else would it be?"

She suddenly sits up on her haunches and gazes around. *What's wrong? Why are you here? Do you need to go somewhere?*

I chuckle. "Relax, Elan. I'm fine. I'm visiting you to see how you are."

But we only just got here. There must be something wrong, or you wouldn't be out here already. I had just fallen asleep. That salve had a real kick to it, and I think it messed with my brain.

"Yes, I heard you sleeping. You snore like a trouper, by the way."

I do not! I sleep like a baby—not a single sound.

"You keep telling yourself that." I pet her patronizingly on the leg. "But I know what I heard." I smile. "Relax. I'm just here for a visit."

She stares at me, the disbelief prominent in her eyes. *Something must have happened. What was it?*

"What? I can't visit an old friend?"

You can. But I know you have Valkyrie friends, as well. They're ones you trust. So why would you come to see me instead of Hildr and Eir? Not that I'm complaining. She adds quickly, *I love your company.*

Exhaling loudly, I stare out into the distance. "Have you ever seen a weird old lady?"

Aren't you old?

I glare at her. "I'm not old."

8

You are compared to me. I'm like, what… two? And you're like… She screws up her face. *Almost eighteen?*

"Almost. But that is still not old, especially for a Valkyrie. You must be feeling better. You're starting to get cheeky again."

Just saying! You know how it is.

I roll my eyes. "When I say old, I mean as in wrinkles everywhere and gnarly hands. Have you seen anyone around here that looks like that?"

No. I haven't. Why are you asking?

"Because something strange happened inside." I look out over the rugged landscape, studying the valley below. The wind catches my hair, blowing its long dark-brown locks across my face. I hook it behind my ear.

Like what? Elan's gaze turns intense as her protective nature surfaces.

"An old woman touched my scarred arm, and a tingling sensation ran down it." I pull my gaze from the valley and rub my arm, staring at my pale, unchanged skin. "It's still tingling."

Maybe you just knocked your funny bone before she touched it, or perhaps you knocked it when you were flying home.

I shake my head. "No. It only happened when we arrived back here, and after the older lady stroked it. She came out of nowhere and touched me right in the middle of Rota, Prima, and Mist attacking me in the bathroom when I was doing my duties. And the worst thing is that my left palm connected with Rota when she was trying to do something mean to me." I stare out into the distance again, trying to let the view take away some of the painful, confusing memory. "The next thing I know, Rota has fallen on the floor, unconscious. It was scary. I didn't even try to do anything." I pause while rubbing my arm absentmindedly. My forehead pushes into a frown. "Do you think there is magic in Asgard?"

Do you think there are gods in Asgard?
Sarcasm fills her voice.

I glare at her with disapproval.

Her face holds innocence. *What? You ask me a question I give you an answer in a query. Is there such a thing as gods in Asgard?* She repeats. *Is there such a thing as dragons talking to Valkyries? My point being that anything is possible. There are many supernatural forces at play.*

The thought tosses through my mind. She's right. By pointing out those two small facts, anything is possible.

But then again, perhaps she just fell and had a seizure. I don't know. She shrugs. *Why don't you touch me with that hand and see if anything happens to me?*

Worry clouds my vision. "I don't want to hurt you."

Tsk, tsk. Oh, please. I'm huge. I'd be surprised if you can do anything to me.

I shrug. "Okay. You asked for it." I place my left hand against her flank and concentrate.

Elan throws her head forward and roars.

- CHAPTER TWO -

Yanking my hand away, I look at her with horror. "Oh, no! I didn't mean to hurt you."

The scales on her forehead pull together in agony. Hearing a noise behind me, I spin around. Her roar must have attracted attention. This is bad. Someone might be coming to capture Elan, and she can't defend herself because I hurt her.

Panic engulfs me when several winged Valkyries take to the sky. From that height, they will find her in no time—she is no longer invisible. I'm torn between telling her to turn invisible and seeing if she's all right.

"I'm so sorry, Elan. Are you all right?" I turn and see that she's invisible, and a wave of relief and confusion sweeps over me.

I'm fine. I was just having you on. She chuckles.

"Elan," I grumble, failing to see the funny side. "That's not funny. I was extremely worried."

I know. It was worth doing it, just to see your expression.

I lightly slap the back of my hand against her invisible form, aiming for her leg. "You're so in trouble. Way to play the guilt trip." I shoot daggers at her with my eyes. "Did you feel anything at all?"

When her chuckling subsides, she says, *I didn't feel a thing. You couldn't have hurt that Valkyrie—nothing came out of your hand. It's got to be your imagination.*

"Then how do you explain her collapsing to the ground and the tingling in my arm?" I ask.

It must've been a coincidence. Rota must've had a seizure or something right after you touched her. It serves her right, really. She shouldn't be treating you like that.

"Yeah. Like you dragons get along so well?" I cross my arms, still annoyed that she faked being hurt and made me worry. I watch as the winged Valkyries fly off in the opposite direction, probably just stretching their wings while checking the grounds and making sure there are no threats in the area.

Strong hues of orange, yellow, and dark blue line the horizon as the sun exits the realm for the night. A deep sadness fills me as I realize that I have to return to the academy. "Elan, what am I going to do?"

What do you mean? Slowly, she turns visible, and I lean against her side.

"The way Rota, Prima, and Mist treated me was horrible. What happens if all the winged Valkyries want to treat me like that?"

You will probably find it is just a rotten few that are going to be mean like that. What you need to do is show how tough you are and how you can stand up to them. She rocks sideways, swaying me slightly. *And I know you've got it in you. That's why we chose you. You have a lot to prove yet. I'm not going to give up that easily.*

Standing in silence, I think about what she said. "You're right, Elan. I need to stand against them like I always have. I need to rise and prove that they are wrong. Just because they've had more combat training than me doesn't make the winged Valkyries better than me." A strange combination of determination and peace fills me. "How are your injuries healing?"

They are still sore, but I can feel the ointment working. Thank you. I should be a lot better by morning and after a good feed. She prods me lightly with her wing. *Enough about me, you should go inside so I can hunt. I'm starving!*

I push off from her side. "You're right. See you later. Remember to keep invisible so Odin can't find you."

She disappears from view as I stroke her on the leg in parting.

I return to the academy, keeping my eyes peeled for any Valkyries who might be pursuing me, including Mistress Sigrun. None come. I walk down the corridor, gaining confidence with each step. Walking toward the dining hall, I pass several winged Valkyries doing nothing more than the usual sneer. The smell of the food wafts my way, and my stomach growls, screaming its protest at having no food since breakfast. I grab a plate and load it up with a charred steak and a side of fries. It's not my healthiest choice, but after being stuck in the wilderness for so long, I feel like some comfort food. I spot Hildr and Eir in the far corner, and I make my way over then sit opposite them.

"Hey, you. Where have you been?" Eir's gentle eyes search me as if looking for problems.

"Have you finished all the chores given to you?" Hildr's green eyes sharpen on me, and she plays with her left ear, which is loaded with piercings.

I swallow the unchewed mouthful, and it struggles to slide down my throat. "I've forgotten about them."

"What?" Hildr cries. "How can you forget? You were just given them."

"I know, but Rota, Prima, and Mist attacked me in the bathroom."

"Pfft. Typical!" Hildr exclaims. "I gather you taught them a lesson, because you look unscathed."

Clenching my teeth together, I grimace. "I don't know what happened. I touched Rota, and she dropped to the floor, unconscious. I panicked and took off the second they released me. I know they are going to blame me."

A chair pushes back, its legs grinding on the marble floor, and a wingless Valkyrie unceremoniously plunks herself down at the head of our table with her plate full of food. The three of us stare at her. She doesn't look familiar, and judging by Hildr's and Eir's reactions, they think the same thing. She tosses her long brown locks over her shoulder and picks a fry off her plate. She crunches on it without looking up.

"Hello." Eir smiles, and her light-brown eyes shine their welcome. "I'm Eir. This is Hildr, and that's Kara." She indicates us with her hand. "Who are you?"

"I'm the new girl." Without gazing up, she shoves another fry in her mouth.

Hildr's auburn eyebrow rises, and a hint of impatience flashes through her green eyes. "Yes. We gathered that because we haven't seen you before. Are you in your first year at the academy?"

"I guess so." She looks up at Hildr and smiles broadly. I think I see amusement flash through her eyes.

Hildr frowns, looking perplexed over the lack of information she is receiving. "Well, you look rather old for a first year in the academy. Are you older than fifteen?"

"No. I'm fifteen." The Valkyrie's head twitches to the side before she shoves another fry in her mouth.

I have never seen a Valkyrie twitch before, and I frown in confusion. She doesn't seem like an ordinary Valkyrie.

"Well, welcome." Eir is the only one of us who smiles broadly.

"Thanks." She pulls a book from her lap, places it on the table, then flicks through the pages.

Hildr casts me a bewildered look. "Look. It's not unlike Kara. She reads everywhere she goes."

"I'm not that bad," I say. "I haven't had a chance to pick up a book in a while. After all, I've been stuck in the wilderness. I'm getting withdrawals."

The new girl ignores us as she munches on some more fries and turns a page. It's weird behavior for a dining hall, but I'm not one to judge constant reading. I've lost count how many times I didn't want to put down a book.

I slide my plate along and scoot closer. "What are you reading?"

She shrugs and continues picking at her food. "Just a book from the restricted section."

"Do you mind if I have a look?" I try to sneak a peek past her hand.

"Yeah. Kara loves books," Eir says.

The girl shrugs, so I shuffle a bit closer and look at the book from the odd angle. The strange tingling sensation runs up my left arm.

I don't know what happened back there in the bathrooms, but my arm hasn't been the same since.

As I gaze down at the book, she flicks the page, and my hand freezes its rubbing, pausing over my upper arm. My mouth drops open.

The newest page shows a picture of the creature that has been flying around Asgard for the last three years—the one that marked my arm and gave me the scar. I point at it in disbelief. "I have seen that creature."

The girl keeps her nose buried in the book and shoves another fry into her mouth. She shrugs and says with her mouth full, "That's a zmey."

"Does it say how many there are? Are they rare?" I edge forward, trying to get a better look.

"I believe this is the only one."

"Does it say anything else?" I search the page from the odd angle, trying to work out the upside-down writing.

"Only that they live for a very long time," she answers, sounding bored.

"Are they normally vicious?" I ask. "I was attacked by one while I was chasing it away from something it was trying to steal."

"They are vicious if they really want something and something stops them from getting it."

I remember how it attacked Heimdall at his gate when I escaped to Midgard. If the creature would only have attacked because it couldn't get to something it was after, it didn't make sense why the creature would attack Heimdall. *Unless...* I stop my thoughts on their tracks.

There is no way the zmey would have done what I thought a second ago. I shake my head. It's a fantasy to think that the creature was purposely distracting him so I could escape from Asgard. "How do you know so much about these creatures?"

The girl shoves another fry in her mouth and gives me a bland look. "Because I read."

I frown then glance at my neglected plate before taking another mouthful of steak and chew it slowly. As much as I love reading and the knowledge it brings, that wasn't a believable explanation. I'm starting to think this girl is hiding something.

- CHAPTER THREE -

Getting the feeling that I'm invading her space, I scoot a seat away from the strange Valkyrie and watch her flick through her book. I am dying to rip the book out of her hands, but that would be an unforgivable crime to a bookworm. She casually turns more pages that reveal all kinds of creatures, some in the shape of humans. I can't quite see the pictures correctly from where I am sitting, but I can't imagine that any of the images would spark my interest like the creature did.

Trying my best to ignore the Valkyrie, I face Hildr and Eir, focusing on my meal.

"Oh. Look who it is." The spite in Hildr's voice carries over the din of the dining hall, and I search over my shoulders, looking for the person drawing her interest.

I spot Rota, with Prima aiding her into the room. Mist follows not far behind, twirling her beautiful blond locks. I swallow my food with difficulty, and the lump sits just under my esophagus. Rota's perfect face is pale under her blond locks, and her eyes are haunted as though she has been pretty shaken up. Prima's eyes narrow as she glances around the room. It is uncanny how all the winged Valkyries look almost the same, with only slight variances that distinguish them. Although their mannerisms often help tell the difference between their perfect faces, blond hair that falls to their shoulders, and majestic white wings protruding from their shoulder blades. The wingless Valkyries lack these things, along with their esteemed uniform of the tan leather jacket and the long, tight medium-blue leather pants.

Seeing Prima assist Rota is a strange sight. Valkyries are supposed to be tough and rarely in need of assistance. Because of this, they are trying to hide the fact that Prima's arm is hooked around Rota as she aids her through the food hall.

"What's wrong with her?" Eir asks. "She almost looks like she's ill."

My tongue lies frozen in my mouth. I don't know what to say. Explaining what happened will be hard.

The new girl looks up from her book. "I hear she was struck by magic today."

The three of us stare at her.

"Magic?" Hildr scoffs. "There is no such thing here, unless you are talking about her pride getting handed to her. That's what I would call magic."

The girl shrugs, her hand still holding the pages. She looks nonchalantly back at the book then at Rota then at me. "You'd be surprised what could be floating around. A single scratch or touch—they could be life-changing."

Her dark-brown eyes bore into me, and a shiver travels up my spine.

"What are you talking about?" Eir asks. "You almost sound as crazy as me."

Hildr scoffs. "Yeah. She's a peacemaker that's living in a Valkyrie academy. Go figure! That is one crazy idea."

The peculiar Valkyrie's eyes do not leave my face, and her hands still clasp the pages of the book. A strange knowing look passes across her face. "It is just as I said. I will let you work that out."

She closes the book and tucks it under her arm with the back cover facing out. Still keen to know the title of the book, I search the cover.

Nothing is written on the back cover or the spine. She stands and walks away without saying a word.

I study every feature of the book as she walks past. I'll have to go search for that one in the library—it has me intrigued. I want to find out more about that creature and if it resides anywhere else or is mentioned anywhere else in the library books. She said it was a zmey. I've never heard of it.

When she is gone, I search for Rota again. Whatever happened to her certainly knocked her about. Valkyries heal quickly, yet she still needs to be aided by Prima.

Eir stares at Rota with concerned eyes. "What did happen to her?"

I weigh my options, wondering how much I should tell them. I can't explain it myself, but these two have been through a lot with me. They have been there supporting my theory on the dragon alliance and befriending dragons. They have even taken it further and have been locked up because of me. I think they deserve an answer, and because of this, I will give them the best I can.

"When I met with Mistress Sigrun, she sent me to clean the bathrooms as one of my penalty chores. Knowing that this chore would be allocated to me, Rota, Prima, and Mist made a disgusting mess throughout the bathrooms. They wanted to watch me clean it up, so they came and, as usual, started fighting me. They even secured me so that they could give me a swirly."

Eir screws up her nose.

Hildr slams her fist on the table, making me jump. "How dare they!"

I nod. "But not just that. While they grabbed me, the old woman that I met in the wilderness walked in and touched me. She said something weird and nicely told them off, and then she walked back out again."

"That is weird." Eir pulls back, looking at me strangely. "You would have thought she could've stepped in and helped, or at least told someone."

I shake my head. "She just walked in and touched me on my arm. The scar the creature gave me a couple of years ago went berserk with tingling, but it plays up now and then, so I didn't think anything of it." I stabbed a fork into my food. "The weird thing is, not long after the old woman left, I touched Rota, trying to defend myself, and she fell to the ground unconscious. None of us know what happened." I throw down the fork, and it clatters against the plate. "Prima dropped her hold on me, and I took one look at Rota. Then I ran. Mist was only worried about looking at herself in the mirror. I guess she thought the other two had it covered." I shrug.

"Where did you go?" Eir asks.

"I ran straight out the door to Elan. I wondered if Rota was hit by magic, but after running it through with Elan, it sounded crazy. So to help me ease my worries, Elan told me to touch her with the same arm and see what happened."

"And what did happen?" Eir takes a sip of water from her glass.

"What do you think happened?" I asked her.

"We don't know." Hildr's freckly face screws up with impatience. "It was only a few days ago that we thought talking to a dragon was impossible."

"Nothing happened. She didn't feel a single thing. So it had to just be the timing. There's obviously something wrong with Rota, and she passed out right when I touched her."

We watch Prima as she sits Rota down and helps with her food. When she finishes looking after her, she sits next to her to eat. Her eyes search the room then land on us. They narrow.

"Now what?" Hildr huffs. "That girl hasn't left us alone since we came back from our flight."

"I don't know." I lean over my plate, no longer interested in my food. Prima doesn't take her eyes off us as she shovels food into her mouth and chomps down hard. I wish she would leave us alone. One day without them annoying us would be a godsend.

My eyes wander over the dining hall. From what I can see, nearly all the Valkyries are in the room, getting their meal. Valkyries are few, and the academy caters only for the younger generation. Because Valkyries are immortal, to stop the population from expanding too much, they are rarely able to bear young.

"How many Valkyries do you think are in the academy?" I ask.

"About forty," Eir says. "There's about ten for each grade."

"Why's that?" Hildr asks.

"Just curious. How many wingless Valkyries are there out of all those?"

Eir counts them on her fingers. "About ten."

"So we're completely outnumbered," I say. "It's like they're the blessed ones and we're the ones that are disabled by the curse of a weird mutation—we lack wings."

"Yeah. That's been obvious from the start. What's your point?" Hildr asks.

"My point is that it is easy to pick on the ones that are fewer in numbers," I say.

"And if your headmistress is constantly putting you down and encouraging the majority..." Hildr's eyes travel to the far corner of the room, and her face screws up with annoyance.

I spin around to see what caught her attention. Mistress Sigrun stands at the entrance of the dining hall. She claps her hands together three times in a loud staccato.

"Attention, Valkyries." She repeats the staccato clap. "I have an announcement to make." Her eyes land directly on me and tighten.

- CHAPTER FOUR -

It takes all my effort to look at her. "What have we done now?" I ask.

"I haven't done anything. Perhaps it's the ones who didn't finish their chores." Hildr nudges me lightly and smirks.

"It wouldn't be the first time." Eir grins with her.

"This is because she gives us so many stupid chores." I slam my back against the chair and cross my arms. "And I'm always in the firing line."

"You're always the one racing off and causing trouble." Eir beams.

"I second that." Hildr grins like a Cheshire cat. "But I have had a taste of it now, and I like it."

"Valkyries! Attention!" Mistress Sigrun calls out again. "I have demanded your silence."

A loud clatter pierces the room as the cutlery hits the plates, and the hall falls into an eerie silence, waiting for Mistress Sigrun to begin.

The mistress tilts her chin to the group, acknowledging the silence. "It has come to my attention that a few wingless Valkyries here think they're more important than the winged Valkyries. So much so that they don't finish their chores." Her eyes circle the room and land on me. "This is not tolerable, and my patience has run thin." She crosses her arms and paces a few steps in front of the doorway.

Her tight leather pants creak with every movement, and the clack of her shoes on the hard floor echoes through the silence. "And no matter how much I try, these Valkyries will not pull into line. And it is appalling." She paces more, then stops abruptly, spinning around to face the Valkyries in the room.

"So today I have come up with a plan. Tomorrow at first light, we are going to set a challenge. For these three wingless Valkyries that think they are better than the winged— and I'm sure you all know who they are, so I'm not going to hide it." Her eyes land on me again. "They will have to prove themselves in a competition." She holds up a finger. "But, to make this fair, even though they don't deserve it, I'm going to choose three winged Valkyries from within the same grade level as their opponents."

The hairs on the back my neck prickle. Mistress Sigrun being fair to wingless Valkyries—that's something I've never seen.

She starts pacing again. "This challenge will have no particular rules. And this challenge will be until the Valkyrie's opponent is wiped out. If it ends in death, then there will be no consequences for the Valkyrie responsible." She smirks, and her wings twitch, making her seem more pompous. "Because we all know which side that will be." She loops her hands behind her back and paces more. "There is one catch. This fight will take place at the top of one of our mountains, and there is only one way down from the top—and that is flying, unless you are a rock climber experienced in free climbing. The only way down besides the path up will be sharp, jagged cliffs. That way, there will be no escaping." Her smirk grows broader, and she lifts her chin. "Well… not for the wingless Valkyries."

"That doesn't seem fair," one of the wingless Valkyries calls out.

Mistress Sigrun glares at her, and the Valkyrie cringes on the spot.

Despite her cowering away, I thought she was quite brave calling out like that. I thought it was only me and my little group who challenged the winged Valkyries. Perhaps there are more of us who would like to prove to the winged Valkyries that they are not superior. This thought alone gives me hope. I know I definitely agree with her. It doesn't seem fair. If we fall, we have no means to save ourselves from our fall. The winged Valkyries, of course, have their wings.

After staring intently at the other Valkyrie, Mistress Sigrun walks over to Rota's table. She squats and chats quietly to Rota. After a while, Rota nods, and Mistress Sigrun rises to her feet and walks back to the entrance of the hall.

"Right. As we all know who the wingless Valkyries are..." All eyes fall on my group. "Kara, Hildr, and Eir, you are the wingless Valkyries."

"And what happens if we win?" I ask Mistress Sigrun, tilting my chin in the air. If I am putting my life at risk, I am doing it with pride and something to fight for.

She glares at me, then her eyes soften with amusement as she dismissively flicks her hand in the air. "Pfft. I guess you'll get some sort of prize."

"What about being able to go to Midgard to help with the reaping of souls for Valhalla?" I call out before she has a chance to offer something insignificant.

She stops in her tracks and turns to me, her face a mixture of shock and displeasure before it morphs into laughter. "Sure. Let's make that your reward." She couldn't have been more condescending. "I know you have no chance of winning anyway. So sure." She holds her stomach and looses a hearty, belly-jerking laugh.

Despite her reaction, I feel elated. There's a chance that I get to go to Midgard without being kicked out.

Mistress Sigrun interrupts my thoughts. "Now these three imbeciles will be going up against the best in their level. If they want to prove that they are the best, then they must go up against the best. They will be going up against Prima, Rota, and Mist. And they cannot whine that they have been hard-done-by because they are even getting an advantage— Rota hasn't been well today and possibly won't be better tomorrow. As much as Valkyries can heal quickly, Rota has been hit with a virus that will take longer than a few hours to disappear." She dusts off the front of her shirt and pulls her tan leather jacket closed. "There, my kindness is done. I have given you inconsiderate wingless Valkyries leeway. And even though Rota is putting her life at risk because she is not in the best of health, she has still agreed to fight. She believes in our cause and the dominance of the winged Valkyries and putting the wingless Valkyries in their place." The mistress walks in a slow, purposeful pace with her chin held high, peering down at all the wingless Valkyries. "Her passion alone will win the fight and ride over any of her illness."

"Oh, what hogwash!" Hildr says only loudly enough for us to hear while thumping her fist on the table. Her face turns a contrasting red to her spikey ginger hair.

"I can't agree with you more." A knot of anxiety and hope twists deep in my stomach.

"Why me?" Eir asks. "I haven't done anything. I just want peace. Sure, I'm friends with you guys and agree with your cause, but I haven't done anything."

"You have. You were born wingless," Hildr says. "To make things worse, you've stuck with us."

Eir sighs. "And you're the best friends, so I wouldn't have it any other way."

Mistress Sigrun claps her hands a few times to silence the room again. "Now remember— first light, people. Anyone who's late is immediately disqualified. And losers… don't be late!" She sneers at us before smiling at Rota, Prima, and Mist then exiting the door.

- CHAPTER FIVE -

When Mistress Sigrun leaves, the room fills with the clatter of cutlery and excited chatter. Distrusting sneers and side glances cut our way.

Eir stabs her food with her fork, but it never makes it into her mouth. After a while, she plonks her fork down. "I'm going to go visit Naga. I haven't had a chance to ride him after we talked. That's something I want to do before I die."

"You're being a bit melodramatic." Hildr plays with the clump of earrings on her left ear. "Our fighting skills are just as good as theirs."

"Yeah, yours and Kara's fighting skills are almost as good as theirs. I can fight, but I hate disrupting the peace. I prefer to talk it through rather than fight."

I place my hand on her back. "We'll work something out. Don't worry." As I say this, I feel like a hypocrite, and my stomach churns. There are no rules. They can force us off the edge of the cliff, and we could fall to our deaths. If we do the same to them, they can fly and return, along with their combat training being much more advanced than ours. The academy has never given the wingless Valkyries the same training poured into the winged students.

I put on a brave face and rub Eir's back. "Then let's go. I like Naga. He's a cheerful fellow. Maybe he can cheer you up."

We push back our chairs and stand before making our way out of the dining hall and to the dragon stalls. As we near the exit of the academy building, someone calls out. "Hey, wait up."

I spin around to find the wingless Valkyrie who had challenged Mistress Sigrun about the unfairness of the challenge. She jogged up to us and stopped. "I want to say that I'm proud of you guys. You do a great job. More of us should stand together and stand up against them. This is my last year at the academy, and no one else would help me stand up against them. It was just me. That's great that you guys are coming through."

"Thanks," I say a bit hesitantly, confused over the sudden attention.

"No problem." She turns to leave before I can ask her name, then pauses. "Oh, by the way, if you're fighting Rota, remember when she goes to do a spinning knockout kick, she leaves herself wide open for a hit. Take stock of that and use it to your advantage."

"Thanks," I say with more enthusiasm. "Any help is great."

"There are no rules. They can play dirty, so you play just as dirty. You need as much advantage as you can, using whatever surprise elements you can muster."

"Thanks. What's your name again?" I ask.

"Britta."

"I am—"

"Kara. You're Hildr and"—she points to Eir—"you're Eir. Yeah, I know who you are. You're starting to be legends amongst the wingless."

My mouth drops open. "Oh. We had no idea. We are just trying to change the attitude of the winged Valkyries."

"I wish you luck. Even if you're not winning against the winged Valkyries, you're starting to get through to the wingless. If they don't watch it, the academy will have an uprising." She slaps Hildr on the shoulders before turning to leave.

We step out into the open air, and the moon paves a path along the valleys of Asgard.

"That was strange," Eir says.

Hildr falls into step with me. "Look what you've done, Kara."

"It's not just me. You're part of this too."

"Please. I've hardly done anything in comparison to you. We got ourselves locked up for a while, that's about it. You did the rest." Her tone is not accusing, merely a voice of encouragement.

"The support you have given me is priceless. And comments like what Britta gave us show there is hope for us all. We need to win this battle tomorrow."

We cross through and follow the path toward the dragon stalls. We reach Naga's stall and roll the stone door aside. Together, we stick our heads through. Naga sits in the corner with his back straight, sitting at attention. His flat head turns, and his eyes land on us. His tail wags.

"Aww! You really are cute, Naga," Eir says as she charges through.

Naga sits still, and his eyes widen as he watches her approach. He seems shocked yet pleased that Eir is charging over to greet him.

He sits still, patiently waiting. His eyes are wide. *Hellos. What… what's happening?*

"We've come to visit you, Naga," I say, and my heart sings as his tail wags some more.

Naga likes visits. Naga wants more.

"And you will get some more." I smile. His inability to speak English correctly makes him more adorable. "Am guessing you don't know, Naga, but Eir wants to connect with you. She wants you to take her for flights and to be her dragon friend."

Naga's eyes widen as his eyes bounce from me to Eir several times before landing on Eir. *Is this truth?*

Eir looks adoringly at the dragon. "Yes, Naga. This is very true. I think you're delightful." She rushes forward and hugs him around the neck. He tilts his flat head, nuzzling into her with his hornless head.

Even when I's got cold and when I's sneeze fire?

Eir smiles. "Yes, Naga. Even when you sneeze fire, only please try to aim them away from me."

I wills try. He jumps to all four feet and jigs in front of her, stretching out his wings and showing off the white dots that look like stars against his blue membrane wings. She giggles, and he charges up to her, slinging his blue body to sit next to her, and accidentally knocks into her. She stumbles and lands on her backside. She jumps to her feet, still giggling, and throws her arms around him, embracing him around the neck and trying to remain on her feet as he laps up her affection. There doesn't seem to be a nasty bone in his body.

After watching them for a few minutes, I interrupt their reunion. "Now, Naga, do you promise to stay in your stall, as per the Dragon Alliance agreement, if I take these cuffs off you?"

Naga nods enthusiastically. *Yes. Yes, I promise I stay.*

"I mean it, Naga." I tilt my head and look at him under a raised eyebrow. "You have to stay here, or else we can get into a lot of trouble because you have run away. Odin becomes very angry when the dragons disappear. He doesn't even like it when they disappear for a little bit and come back. But I would like to free you to see you roam a little bit."

I be good, Naga says quickly. *I promise.*

Gazing deep into Naga's eyes, I can see he is telling the truth. He has such an innocence about him that makes him adorable. I run my hand over his flat head then circle to his back leg secured with the chain. I fish for my skeleton key, stick it into the lock, and move it around until the lock clicks and the chain pops open.

Why you doing this? Naga asks.

"Because tomorrow, we have to face our enemies in the Valkyrie Academy."

Eir goes in and cuddles him around his neck to mother him some more. She lets him go then looks at us. "I am so worried about tomorrow. My stomach is doing little flips."

"The Valkyrie back at the academy is right. There are no rules. We can do whatever we want to them." Hildr stands with her legs in a fighting stance as if preparing for tomorrow.

"But they can do whatever they want to us too, and that includes pushing us over the side." Eir strokes Naga down his blue neck, and his eyes look at her adoringly. "We cannot fly. It's not fair. Tomorrow could be our last day to live."

Naga's eyes widen. He nudges into her, and she obliges by hooking her arm around his neck, cuddling him close.

"At least I got to come and be with you, little guy." Eir presses her face into his neck. "That made my day. It is one of the things I wanted to do before I died."

Naga pulls back and looks at Eir with wide blue eyes. *My English no good. But Naga think that you sad. I thinks you say you die.*

Eir returns his gaze with serious eyes. "That is possible, Naga. Tomorrow morning, at first light, we have to fight the winged Valkyries." She sits on a rock and cups her hands in her lap, playing with her fingers. "And I'm scared."

Then don't fight, he says.

"We have to, Naga. We don't have a choice. Really, this is a competition that they're making us do because they want to kill the three of us. It all started because of what we did with the dragons—because Hildr took a dragon for a ride and Kara saved Elan from Odin's captivity. Now they want to make us pay."

- CHAPTER SIX -

*T*he next morning, a horn blasts me from my sleep. My eyelids fling open, and my first impression is that it's a call to Midgard for another war. The room is dark, and the sun has not yet risen. The horn sounds again, and I realize that the sound is different from the usual Midgard call. It must be a call for the fight this morning. As I stare across the room, the realization hits me—we are running out of time. I reach over my bed for my bedside table and rub the glow rock, and it illuminates. The light shines on the pale faces of Hildr and Eir. It has been a restless night's sleep for all of us, tossing and turning, in anticipation of what is going to happen. I swing my legs over the side of the bed, and my feet fall to the floor. I rub the sleep from my eyes and stretch my arms to the ceiling.

"I'm not ready for this." Eir's mouth is downturned, and she almost looks depressed.

"Eir, you have to stop being so negative," Hildr snaps. "I know you're a peacekeeper and all, but you can do it. We've seen you fight. When you're on a roll, you're an excellent fighter. It's only your mental attitude toward peace that stops you from winning sometimes. You need to remember that there are no rules and that they may kill us."

Eir's shoulders sag in defeat. "I know. I have to put on my tough face."

The horn blows again, and Hildr complains, "What, we don't even get breakfast?"

I rise to my feet. "Clearly not. Although I don't know if I could keep anything down right now." I start pulling on the black fighting leathers of the wingless Valkyries. I grab my favorite quiver of arrows and shove my sword between the quiver and my back. I hook my sling on the back of my pants. I've always loved that sling, ever since it helped defend me in the wastelands against the creature I now know is called a zmey. I run an appreciative hand over the rough texture of the sling's material. That day holds so many memories, and it was the start of my involvement with Elan.

I slide on my boots and run my fingers through my long dark-brown hair. "I'm going to grab a roll on my way past the kitchen anyway."

"I'm coming too," Hildr says.

We pass by the kitchen, grabbing a roll, and I grab one for Eir and hand it to her.

"Gee, thanks," she says half-heartedly. She tucks it inside the pocket of her black jacket. "I'll eat it later. Right now, my stomach is a mess of knots. I think I'll get through by adrenaline alone."

We step outside of the academy walls, and someone grabs me from behind. I spin to see the strange girl from the dining room with the curious book. The girl's hand grasps my left arm, and a strange look is plastered over her face. Yanking backward, I try to release her grip, but it doesn't give. Tingling, stronger than it was before, shoots down my arm. She must have stirred up the injury. I tug again, and this time, her grasp releases. Without saying a word, she spins and leaves.

"That's odd." Eir's expression is confused as she watches the girl leave.

"You're telling me!" I shake my head and rub my arm.

We turn away from her and walk a few feet around the corner of the academy, where we meet Mistress Sigrun and a couple of winged Valkyries.

"It's about time you arrived." She plants her fists against her hips. "I was about to charge into your room and drag you out myself. We thought you were trying to skip it."

"Good morning to you too, mistress." I smile cheerfully, hiding my nerves. "Where are we heading?"

She glares at me then spins around, aiming her finger at the highest peak. The flat surface at the top of the mountain is barely visible.

"How are we going to get there, mistress?" Eir asks as all the remaining color drains from her face. "It even looks impossible to free climb that mountain."

The leader of the academy looks down her nose at Eir. "I was going to make you climb up the rocks, but that would make us wait too long for a wingless. Instead, the winged Valkyries are going to be doing all the work for you again. Not just one, but two winged

Valkyries will have to be put out. Unfortunately, we need one for each side to carry you up there."

"How considerate of you, mistress." Hildr's fist opens and closes at her side.

Mistress gives Hildr a sharp look, noting the sarcasm in Hildr's voice. "Yes, it is. Yet you wingless still don't treat us with respect," she says. "The winged Valkyries do so much for your kind."

Suddenly, strong hands grab both my arms and hook underneath them. Before I know it, I'm rising off the ground and into the air. My stomach lurches over the harsh treatment without warning.

I'm flanked by winged Valkyries with beautiful blond hair flicking behind their shoulders as they fly. Their majestic wings beat powerfully, pulling me into the air. Their pale, beautiful faces focus on the top of the mountain. It is a vast rise to the top. If we fall, it will definitely be to our deaths.

Neither of them says a word as they fly toward the top—my only comfort is the monotonous beat of their wings. I try hard not to glance down. Riding a dragon would be safer than being carried by two winged Valkyries. There is just so much more security on the back of a dragon, feeling that vast size and power underneath my body.

My stomach reels over the lack of security, churning so much that it takes all my mental effort not to throw up. To pull my thoughts away from the possibility, I search for Eir and Hildr. I hear the flapping wings behind us, and I assume that it's winged Valkyries carrying the other two behind me, but they are out of my sight.

The rugged terrain sinks beneath us, and the journey seems endless. Even with their powerful strokes, it takes quite some time to rise to the top of the mountain. Finally, we reached the edge of the top of the mountain, and my feet fold underneath me when the winged Valkyries drop me to the ground. They aren't even gentle when they set me down.

The sun peeks over the horizon, bathing the land of Asgard in a golden glow. Opposite me across the other side of the flat top, Rota, Prima, and Mist stand ready, their faces screwed up in their usual scowls. My eyes travel farther, and I notice that winged Valkyries from the academy surround the plain. They hover in a circle formation around the edges. The sun's beautiful light casts eerie shadows on their faces. Because of the location of the fight, there is not one wingless Valkyrie among the spectators. They will not be able to watch the fight and see if it is fair. Again, they are excluded. Here we are, fighting for their rights, and they can't even watch and support us.

A thump sounds on my left, and I turn to find Hildr's Valkyrie escorts have unceremoniously dumped her, as well. Then they push up into the sky and join the other winged Valkyries circling the plain. Another thump catches my attention, and I look to my right to see Eir being given the same treatment before her escorts also join the other spectators.

Hildr's hand hovers over the hilt of her sword as she eyes each spectating Valkyrie. "What's stopping them from joining in, as well?" She nods, indicating the live circle. "There is nobody to witness that they have cheated, and it wasn't an even match of three against three. Naturally, the winged Valkyries are going to stick up for their own if this fight turns sour for them."

My cheeks turn clammy as I stare up into the glaring blue eyes. There is a significant element of truth to Hildr's words. There is no one to witness any unfairness, and there is nowhere that we can go to escape it. I don't see even one friendly face.

"I want this to be over with already," Eir says. "If we win this—"

"*When* we win this," Hildr interrupts.

Eir rolls her eyes. "Okay. When we win, we need to teach this bunch of hypocrites a lesson."

"Well, they sound like fighting words." One side of Hildr's mouth lifts in a smirk. "As far as I'm concerned, I'm ready to start now." She positions her legs, planting her feet shoulder width apart, with one foot in front of the other, and sliding metal rings as she draws out her sword. She holds it above her head.

As I mimic her with my sword, the sound of sliding metal resonates, followed by an echo to my right as Eir does the same.

"Bring it on!" Hildr says through gritted teeth.

- CHAPTER SEVEN -

A sharp whistle blows, and all eyes focus on the newly arrived mistress of the academy.

"Get ready… Go!" Her voice carries over the distance before she blows the whistle and it screams through the air.

At first, my feet remain fixed as I study the circling Valkyries to see what they will do. When I am confident they are not about to interfere, I loose a pent-up breath. This may be a fair fight after all—at least for now. Rota,

Prima, and Mist edge toward us. We imitate them from our side—all three of us together approach at the same speed. Our arms remain ready, with our swords drawn.

My arm tingles, and I try to shake it out. The tingling is frustrating, always doing this at the most inconvenient times. Despite the burning urge to rub away the tingling, I can't spare the hand holding the sword. I just have to let the sensation run its course.

A gust of wind blows the dark strands of hair over my face, and I hook it back behind my ear. In the excitement to leave the room, I forgot to tie it out of the way. I curse my absentmindedness. There is nothing worse than fighting with hair obscuring the view.

I shake my head. I can't believe I just thought that. The last thing I need to do is think about hair when I'm about to go into battle. *Way to go, Valkyrie! You're showing the true signs of a warrior,* I chastise myself sardonically.

My attention careens to Eir. Her hair is pulled back into a ponytail that falls down her back. Beads of sweat pearl on her face, and it glistens in the early-morning sun.

"You'll do good, Eir." I try to offer words of encouragement.

She nods in a jerky, unsure movement as her eyes remain focused on the three approaching Valkyries. Mist stands directly opposite her. This is a stroke of luck. I think they will be a better match. Mist is usually too worried about her looks to focus on fighting properly.

In the middle, directly opposite me, is Rota. Her face is paler than usual, giving her the appearance of a porcelain doll. The crisp morning air brings a slight rose to her cheeks, making her look healthier than she did the night before. Her eyes hold a subtle wariness as she moves closer to me. I find this strange. She seriously can't be regarding me as though I hit her with magic yesterday. No Valkyrie has magic.

My arm tingles again, and I try to shake it out. Rota's eyes flick to my arm and widen with fear. I shake my head, trying to clear my vision. I can't be seeing what I think I am. Rota is a fantastic fighter and a formidable opponent. If I beat her, I would be doing well. Fear churns in my stomach, and I pull extra motivation from the reminder of the prize. If we win today, Mistress Sigrun will have to let the three of us go to the fields in Midgard when they are reaping souls. I'm going to hold her to that. After all, she said it in front of the whole academy.

On my side, Prima is eyeing Hildr. These two are a good match. Hildr is a strong fighter, but Prima has had more training. Usually, what Hildr lacks in skills, she makes up for in determination. Hopefully, today will prove to be the same.

A soft whistle pierces the air, and it pulls my attention back to the fight. I turn just in time to see an arrow heading in Eir's direction. She swings her sword while dodging to the side and cuts the shaft in half. It falls to the ground, broken in two. She spins back to the three approaching, and her eyes land on Mist, who has another arrow nocked in her bow, taut and ready to be shot toward Eir. Mist doesn't even wait until we approach and reach each other before starting to fight. I find this rather unbecoming and rude. But then, Mistress Sigrun did say that there are no rules in this fight.

Another arrow flies Eir's way. Without a moment's hesitation, she darts to the side and swings the sword, timing the slice perfectly to slash it in half. Mist reaches her arm over her head and pulls another arrow from her quiver. She starts to nock it in her bow, aiming directly at Eir. Quickly, I search the ground and find the perfect-sized stone, and I scoop it up while unhitching my sling at the same time. I slide the stone in the rough material and fling it around my head. I let the rock fly, hitting Mist on the head. Her hand shoots to her head as she cries out in pain and drops her bow and arrow. Her eyes narrow when they land on me and spot the sling in my hand.

Technically, she's not my opponent at the moment, but I wasn't going to let that stop me. She's not playing fair. She rubs her head and shakes it. When she pulls her hand away, there's a nasty welt not far from her temple. My heart dances between beats. My aim has improved during my last couple of years at the academy. I chuckle inwardly. Mist won't be happy that there is a mark on her beautiful face. She will scowl every time she looks in the mirror until that bruise heals.

Mist pulls her sword out of its sheath, charging toward me. Eir darts in front of me and blocks her path, clashing her sword against Mist's. That was a gutsy and aggressive move for Eir, and my heart swells with pride that she would do that to stop Mist from attacking me. She may be a peacekeeper, but she is loyal to the end. That is one of the things that attracted me to be her friend—plus the fact that she puts up with me.

After seeing Eir dart in and start a sword fight before any of us, Hildr charges forward, aiming straight for Prima and stopping her from helping Mist against Eir. Clanging metal rings out as swords clash as the receiving Valkyries block each attack. Several blows are delivered at the other, slicing and chopping, trying to be the first one to succeed with a hit. Hildr swings her sword, knocking Prima's aside. She retreats in time to swing it in a different direction for another attack. Prima pulls her stomach in, and the sword skims lightly across her torso, the tip slicing open her white T-shirt. I hold back a cry of delight. Hildr was so close to connecting. As intrigued as I am by Hildr's fighting skills, I must pull my focus away and concentrate on my own opponent.

My eyes connect with Rota's, and that strange tingling runs down my arm again, reminding me what happened yesterday. This incident is frustrating me. Despite being impossible, it's like my brain refuses to believe that Rota's collapse was just a coincidence. It wants to think that something did charge out of my hand. After all, I did feel a funny tingling sensation charge down my arm right as it happened yesterday. *Didn't I?*

I shake my head and flail my arm, hooking my sling back onto my pants and grasping the hilt of my sword firmly. Slowly, I maneuver forward, each step sliding and cautious. Rota watches me intensely, her eyes flashing down to my shaking arm, and her eyes widen. Perhaps it is something the old lady did when she spoke to her yesterday. Maybe it was the old lady's actions that made Rota believe something happened to my arm. It was a strange coincidence. It has me baffled, but I have to push this aside for now.

Rota pulls her eyes away from my arm and focuses on my face. From training, I know that she is also skimming my posture with her peripheral vision, watching for my first move. Concentrating on my eyes is also the perfect way for her to steel her emotions and make herself focus, ready for the fight. Her training and practice are starting to manifest. Her other hand creeps up to the hilt of the sword, and she embraces it with two hands. Her eyes are flat and determined—all emotions cleared from her focus.

Oh, Vanir! It is about to start. She is definitely ready to attack. I try to mimic what she is doing. It's difficult. I am not a seasoned warrior. Even though I've had several training sessions, it is nothing compared to what Rota has done, including practice on the fields. Nothing teaches more than a life-and-death fight. Rota and the winged Valkyries have had much practice against the angels of death and any other creatures that decide to attack them while they are out in the fields.

The sound of metal clanging against metal rings out on both sides of me. It takes all my strength to ignore the urge to see if Hildr and Eir are okay. I must focus completely on Rota. I blink, only to open my eyes and see Rota swinging her sword directly at me.

- CHAPTER EIGHT -

My vision tunnels, and the high-pitched sound of clanging swords pierces my eardrums. I move just in time to block Rota's sword from slicing me. My heart thumps rapidly. She pulls back and swings again, the sword careening down, aiming for my head. Thankfully, my training kicks in, and I swing my sword, blocking it just in time. I have to pull my thoughts together. Britta's words enter my thoughts. I blink and notice Rota's underarms are wide open as our swords are locked.

I twist and land a side kick to her ribs. She lurches forward with a groan, pulling her sword down and narrowly missing my leg. As she pulls herself together, her thoughts play out on her face. Then she lunges forward, swiping at me with her sword. I block it, and she retreats then instantly attacks from the other side. I twist and block it with my sword again. These maneuvers repeat as if we are playing a fencing game, swords clashing every time and no one getting through. Weariness swamps my muscles, and my arms ache, making each block or strike a more difficult feat. She pulls her sword away after another of our clashes and swings it horizontally in my direction. My exhausted muscles react too slowly, and the sword slides past my defense. The pain soars through my body, screaming from my torso where the blade connected. My eyes widen, but my vision narrows into a tighter tunnel. Clenching my teeth together, I do my best to pull it together and ignore the pain. I can't let this get to me. Otherwise, it'll distract me from my fight, and things will get worse.

Fear surges through me as I worry about the depth of the injury and the pain it causes me. I grit my teeth and push it aside. Gripping my sword, I swing again. She blocks it, and I spin quickly, striking up from the other direction, knocking her sword aside and nicking up her arm. The sleeve of her tan leather jacket splits open. Her crimson blood runs down her sleeve and stains her medium-blue leather pants. She stumbles back, glancing at her arm, and the icy confidence in her eyes wavers when she looks back at me.

Darting forward, I slice again, but her sword blocks my strike just in time before she stumbles backward a few steps. Seeing her hesitation fuels me forward. I lurch, chopping the sword down at her, and she darts out of the way.

Clanking rings out on either side of me, like music to my ears. Both Eir and Hildr are still fighting, although I am not game to see if they are injured.

The Valkyries around the edge start clapping and cheering, calling out the names of the winged Valkyries. They continue framing our circle, flapping in unison like a grand parade. I wonder how such beautiful creatures can be so mean, then I remind myself that Valkyries are bred to be ruthless and aggressive. We are meant to be warriors first, trained to choose who should live for Valhalla and who should die. Sympathy will only muddy the decision. That is the training of a winged Valkyrie, anyway, and this is what we have to contend with.

Hearing the Valkyries cheer on the winged Valkyries spurs my determination. I slash and swing with so much ferocity and force that

Rota backs away. Before I realize, I have pressed her to the other side of the plain. A gasp travels from the bottom of the mountain. I can't imagine it being possible because it is so far below—unless the wind is carrying the voice. But there is no way that they could know what is happening up here. They can't see what is going on. But one thing is for sure— hearing the wingless Valkyries is inspirational enough. They are waiting for us to win so that they, too, may prove that we are worth more than they give us credit for.

I dart forward with my sword tip pointing at Rota, and she backs off. Then her feet slip. She uncoils her wings and flaps, stopping herself from falling—exercising the unfair advantage that we do not have. She hovers in the air for a moment then dives down toward me. I strike out again. She swerves at the last second, narrowly missing the edge of my sword.

Eir gasps to my right, and I want to see what is happening, but it is too risky to check. I hope she's okay. Rota swoops down, and I spin out of the way, swiping my sword at her. I feel it connect with her skin and drag down her side. Her cry of pain reaches my ears. Her first injury is already mostly healed, just like mine. Healing is the gift of being a Valkyrie, especially for simple wounds like sword wounds.

With blood tarnishing her torso, she dives at me again, and I spin, managing to dodge the strike and catch sight of Hildr. From my glance, I think she is okay. I spin farther, catching sight of Eir to see her balancing just on the edge of the cliff face. Mist has backed her into a corner, attacking her from flying positions just as Rota has attacked me. Eir swings her sword, managing to scratch Mist along her face. Mist's eyes cloud over with anger. Again, she has been injured where it can wound her vanity.

Instantly, her posture changes, overtaken by aggression. She spins around, flicking her wings forcefully before she charges at Eir, spooking her backward. Eir's heel clips a boulder, and she stumbles over the edge of the cliff. A scream crescendos as Eir struggles to find something to grasp. But there is nothing. Her body falls over the edge, and her hands fail to find purchase. Her loud scream pierces the valley, echoing up to the mountaintop.

I scream, "Nooo!"

At the same time, Rota has another go at me. I spot her coming and feel the anger welling up inside. I let the emotion soar through me, pouring into every part of my body. It sparks the tingling down my left arm. The sensation grows stronger each second, making my arm feel as though it is about to explode. Raising my left arm, I hold my hand out to fend off Rota, and it connects with her body as she collides with me. I deflect her sword with mine, and an explosion shoots through my left palm and into her body. Rota's body is flung back, and I watch in amazement and horror as her eyes turn lifeless. She crashes to the ground, her wings crumpling beneath her.

My mouth drops open, and I look at my left hand. Confusion roars through my head as I try to figure out what is going on. I wish I could talk to someone about this. I wish someone could tell me what is going on. The shock consumes me, and I look blankly down at Rota's body on the ground. I don't want to become a killer, but I don't know if I have already crossed that line. I'm not sure what this hand is doing. This time there was a definite surge of power. I throw my hands on my head. Emotion overcomes me. Eir has just fallen to her death, and I may have just become a killer.

A thud sounds beside me, followed by another thud. The fog clouding my mind refuses to clear. Another thud hits the ground not far away, then several more. Removing my hands from my head, I manage to clear enough of the emotional fog to look around. My jaw drops, and my eyes widen. Arrows are embedded deep in the ground surrounding me and have somehow narrowly missed me. Other arrows lie uselessly on their sides. I spin, searching for the culprit. Catching sight of another flying arrow, I am appalled but not completely shocked when I see the flying arrow coming directly from the Valkyrie circle above the plain. Every second Valkyrie has an arrow pointed directly at me, nocked and ready to be set free. More arrows hit the ground around me, and I'm completely encircled with embedded arrows.

A scream disrupts my shock, and I gaze over to see an arrow implanted in Hildr's shoulder. She stumbles backward, nearing the edge of the cliff. I cry out and run toward her, hoping to catch her before she topples over the side, but I'm too far away. Hildr doesn't seem to notice me, and her feet continue their dangerous retreat. I dig in my toes and sprint, ignoring the arrows slamming into the ground around me.

I don't understand how I haven't been hit. Perhaps I am moving too fast. I can hear footsteps behind me, but all my energy is focused on rescuing Hildr. She is reaching the edge way too fast. A fresh round of arrows surround Hildr, and she stumbles.

I cry out—tears already filling my eyes, making it hard to see. "Nooo!"

I can't lose another friend. My hands reach out, trying to grasp her… but I fear it is too late.

- CHAPTER NINE -

My feet won't stop as I continue dashing forward, trying to grasp Hildr. I'm too late. She's already over the edge before I get there. Eventually, somehow, I manage to tell my feet to stop only a few feet away from the edge, before I tumble down after her. Despair hits me as I realize I have arrived just in time to see her topple out of my sight. Her freckled face is white, and her green eyes are wide with horror.

My heart breaks. I can't do anything. I can't fly. I can't run down and save her.

We are surrounded by Valkyries that fly, but not one of them dives down to grab her. Not one of them grabbed Eir, either. Eir's as well as Hildr's deaths are too much to bear. Tears blur my vision, and my shoulders slump. I am crushed. There is no will to go on.

Britta's and Elan's faces fill my thoughts, giving me the will to continue, just as I hear the sound of a sword being drawn. It slices the air, and I spin around, my automatic defenses kicking in. I block Prima's attack with the clash of our swords. With my right hand busy with the sword, I spin around backward and land my left palm straight on her stomach. A burst shoots out of my palm straight into her torso, just as it did to Rota. All the pent-up aggression and emotion rebounds from the top of my arm and out my hand. Barely seeing through my tear-filled eyes, I watch Prima's eyes widen then drain of life. She crumples to the ground, her head slamming against a rock, and her wings fall over the top of her as she lands face first. Arrows thud into the ground around me, surrounding me again, yet not one hits me. I can't for the life of me understand why. These are expert marksmen.

With the shock of recent events catching up to me, I blink a few times and look around. The arrows are definitely flying down. A large double-edged circle of arrow shafts sticking out of the ground surrounds me. I blink a few more times, thinking that this may register where I have been hit—for surely I have been hit by now, but I'm just too numb to realize it. Except I don't feel any pain. Several more arrows are locked in position, ready to be set loose in my direction.

A cloud pulls out from in front of the sun, releasing its light and bathing the ground. Yet a shadow surrounds me. I frown and look up. Nothing is above me.

A movement catches my eye in my peripheral vision. Mist is approaching quickly, another arrow nocked. As I watch her, I am almost ready to give up. Everything I have worked for has failed. All my efforts to prove wingless Valkyries are worth as much as winged are futile. To make things worse, my best friends in the entire academy have just fallen off the edge to their deaths. This is not a fair fight. It was supposed to be three against three, not thirty against three.

I blink the tears from my eyes again, letting the warmth run freely down my face, and look at all the faces of the winged Valkyries hovering above me with their arrows nocked. My eyes land on Mistress Sigrun. She doesn't have a bow in her hand. This is surprising, but on her face is a large smirk of victory. She lifts her chin and looks down her nose at me. The arrows continue to fall, and I still don't understand why they are missing me. I spread my arms and gaze up at the sun. It is uncovered by the cloud, and still, a strange shadow covers the top of me.

Mist takes a few more steps toward me, and slowly, a glimmer of gold grows around me and towers over the top of me like a massive building with four golden pillars holding it up. I glance up and realize that I'm staring at Elan's belly. She is so big that I can fit underneath her chest, and she hovers protectively over me, sheltering me from the arrows. Her head shoots forward, and she roars in Mist's direction. Mist freezes on the spot, her eyes opening wide with terror.

She moves to back up until a thud sounds behind her. Drogon has landed, blocking her escape. He is not as big as Elan, but he is still intimidating, with a head full of horns, especially when he bares his teeth like that. He roars at Mist, shooting fire in her direction, then faces the Valkyries hovering above and does the same. When they shoot another round of arrows, he traces the circle with his plume of fire. The fire does not reach them, but the message is loud and clear.

As I watch him, my heart melts. He will be heartbroken when he finds out about Hildr. He was too late.

A strange slapping sound reaches my ears from behind me. I walk underneath Elan, ducking under her tummy, and peer over the edge from underneath her protection. A blue flash darts through the sky, going from Valkyrie to Valkyrie, knocking them from the hovering circle. As it continues passing through the Valkyries, I focus on the blue flash. I almost squeal with delight when I realize that it is Naga, purposely flying headfirst into each Valkyrie. He is walloping them as if they were balls, and they are having trouble righting themselves. If they try to avoid him, he darts in from a different direction, knocking them in different spots. His face fills with glee, and he is so joyful that for the first time all day, I feel the urge to laugh. My joy is short-lived when I remember that my friends were knocked over the edge to their deaths. It is going to break my heart to tell him. In fact, both dragons will be heartbroken in just moments.

Naga continues his game, and I can hear the Valkyries' bones cracking. Mistress Sigrun sees him coming and darts out of the way, a look of superiority filling her face.

She calls out, "You have not won, wingless. There is still one standing."

I gawk at her in disbelief—I cannot believe she is saying this. This has been such an unfair fight until now. Knowing I can't let her win, I steel myself, ready to head back and fight. I have come so far. I have to pull myself together and end this—otherwise Hildr and Eir will have lost their lives for no reason.

Grabbing my sword from the ground, I head in Mist's direction. I stop when a dragon's tail flings out and knocks Mist off her feet. Her legs fly up in the air, and she topples, hitting her head hard against a rock, knocking her unconscious.

Lifting his chin to the sky, Drogon's big brown face focuses on the mistress and snarls. *The last one standing is Kara. I dare you to challenge it.*

Mistress Sigrun glares down at us, and she looks as though she is about to disagree, but Drogon stands on all fours and flings his head forward, breathing out a large plume of fire right in the direction of the mistress. *That is my last warning,* Drogon roars.

Mistress Sigrun's gaze travels from Drogon to Mist then to me before finishing with Elan. She flaps her wings and takes to the sky, followed by the rest of the conscious winged Valkyries, leaving Mist, Prima, and Rota lying unconscious on the ground. They don't even care for their prized Valkyries enough to pick them up and take them back to the healer.

Elan moves to my side and sits down. *Are you all right?*

I nod then shake my head. "No. Both my friends have died." Tears cloud my vision and plow warm paths down my cheeks, and I drop to my backside. "I have to tell Drogon and Naga." Cloaked in depression, I search for the dragons, but I can't see them anywhere. "Where did they go?"

Elan doesn't answer me, and I turn to ask her again. I spot a small smile creeping onto her face, exposing a couple of her pointiest teeth.

I frown. "Why are you smiling?"

I think you'll find things are not as bad as they seem.

"No, they are worse. I have lost my two best Valkyrie friends and have a treacherous, lying, and conniving nasty leader."

That you have. But your friends—

A thud cuts her off, and I turn to see brown legs standing next to me. My eyes travel up to a face that is full of joy, and I can't for the life of me understand why, especially when my heart is broken by the sad news that I have to tell him.

I can't let it wait any longer. "Drogon, I—" My shoulders sag.

"Oh, Vanir! That was awesome!"

I glance up and see Hildr climbing off Drogon's back. My mouth drops open in disbelief. "Hildr?"

"In the flesh, baby." Her freckles have faded as her face is flushed with excitement.

"But you fell off the side…"

She winces and holds her shoulder. "I did. But Drogon caught me. I'm just dropping by to see if you're all right. Then I'm heading straight to Anita. This arm is killing me."

My heart flutters, and I smile at Drogon before dashing forward to hug Hildr. "I'm sure it is. You have no idea how glad I am to see you alive."

A lighter thump sounds next to me, and I turn to spot Naga. His tail is swinging happily as though he is ready to play.

I crossed my fingers behind my back before I let my eyes travel up to Naga's back. I squeal in delight. Sitting on Naga's back, Eir looks pale, yet she is smiling. I run forward, and she slides down to the ground.

I throw my arms around her. "Oh Vanir! I was certain you two were dead. I'm so happy."

"Not only that, we kicked their butts, girl." Hildr barges in from the outside, hugging us around the shoulders.

- CHAPTER TEN -

My heart swells with joy. "I'm so glad you guys are here." Turning to Elan, I say, "Thank you for protecting me from all those arrows. I couldn't understand why they were missing me."

Of course. I will always protect you. She drops her head down to my level and nudges me with my nose. Her sharp scales catch on my clothes.

I unhook the leather from her scales and lean into her snout, caressing her briefly. "How did you guys know about this and when to come?"

She raises her head and gazes at Naga. *You did have a full conversation in front of Naga. His English may not be so good, and he may not be the brightest dragon, but he certainly understood that you were in danger.* She shows off her full display of teeth in her vicious smile. *The moment you left him last night, he flew out of his cell and warned me, then I visited Drogon. We got together at first light to see what would happen. We didn't know if there were any rules involving dragons or not. But after seeing how the winged Valkyries on the sides attacked, as well, we gathered there were no rules.* She pauses, and the scales between her horns clump together. *It is utterly unfair for all those winged Valkyries to fire upon you when it should be three against three. They already had an advantage. They didn't need to cheat.*

"Technically, it isn't cheating when there are no rules." Hildr's face screws up with contempt. "Now we need to see if Mistress Sigrun carries through with her promise to let you go to Midgard, Kara. After the way they cheated here today, I wouldn't be surprised if she reneges on that too."

Eir scowls. "She better not. That was an agreement made in front of the whole academy. Surely she must have to stick to that. It was even made in front of the other wingless Valkyries."

"Only time will tell." The knife of the traitor twists deeper in my stomach, yet determination pushes me onward. I look at the three dragons. "I'm glad you're here, not only because you saved us, but also because we need a lift down this massive mountain. Can we get a ride, please?"

Of course. We'd love to help, Elan says, her voice back to its normal cheerful tone.

"What about them?" Eir points to Rota, Prima, and Mist. "We can't just leave them here unconscious, even though the winged Valkyries have."

I'll flick them off the side. Drogon stomps toward Prima. *It would be my pleasure.* He takes a few more steps.

Drogon! Elan calls. *You can't do that!*

Yeah, I can. They didn't fight fair, so we shouldn't play fair with them. Besides, they have wings.

But they're unconscious, Drogon. Elan scowls. *If we do something like that, we will never get this alliance sorted. The Valkyries will want to be our enemies forever.*

Drogon huffs, and smoke billows out of his nostrils. He tosses his head aside. *Oh. All right.* He stops in his tracks.

Good choice, Drogon, Elan chirps. *Now, let's get these three down and get them healed.* She gives me a sideways glance. *And you and I are going to discuss what's going on with that arm.*

"I wish I knew." I climb onto Elan's back and hook my legs around her neck.

I'm sorry I didn't have time to grab the saddle. And besides, it is a bit hard for me to be invisible when it is on my back, Elan calls over her shoulder.

"After everything you've done for me today, this is the last thing I'm worried about." I slide my hand gently under her scales and touch the soft skin underneath. "Thank you, Elan."

Always my pleasure. Now I've paid you back once.

I roll my eyes. "I never expected you to pay me back for anything, Elan, but thank you." She pushes off the ground, and Drogon and Naga follow with Eir and Hildr on their backs. When we land, I escort them to see Anita.

The dragons push off and into the sky to collect the winged Valkyries still at the top of the mountain. Despite everything they've been through and seen, they're still doing the right thing, and my heart fills with pride. I don't know how I've ended up being so lucky—just because I saved her egg a couple of years ago.

I escort Hildr and Eir to Anita and assist them onto the gurney table, and they wait for Anita, who is busy in the other room.

"Will you guys be all right if I take off for a bit?"

"I think we will be all right in the healer's hands." Hildr screws up her nose.

"I don't know, Hildr. She could be after us, just like the winged ones," Eir says with a smirk.

I rub Eir's shoulder. "I'm pretty sure you will be safe here."

"I know," she says without the slightest hint of apprehension.

Leaving the healer's quarters, I head to the library. I'm determined to find out if I can find anything about that zmey creature and what's going on with my arm.

I press through the double stone doors into the library. It is several stories high, with books lining every wall up to the ceiling. Surprisingly, ladders are supplied for anyone who doesn't have wings, which is a nice change and a strange sight for the Valkyrie academy. But it all makes sense when I turn to the counter and spot the wingless Valkyrie in charge of the library. A librarian is undoubtedly a better job than a cleaner. It may not be as esteemed as a healer, but in my eyes, it's a valuable position.

Instead of searching on the shelves, I go straight to the librarian. Her thin frame is curved over the bench, and a veil of chin-length black hair hides her face as she leans over a book. I reach the counter, and she turns the page and hooks a strand of hair behind her ear. She looks up, and I can't help but notice her eyes wander over my shoulder in search of reassurance that I don't have wings. I suspect it is an old habit from her days at Valkyrie Academy. She smiles broadly, accentuating her Valkyrie beauty.

"Morning, Jannika."

"Kara, I haven't seen you for a couple of weeks. How can I help?" She even sounds keen to help—a nice change from the day I've had so far.

"I'm looking for a book that has weird creatures in it."

"Are you talking about Asgard or any of the other realms? That's a lot of books to cover. Can you be more specific?"

"I'm looking for one creature in particular. I have only seen it in Asgard a few times. Someone said it is called a zmey."

Creases form on her brow as she frowns in thought, and her lips push to the side. "I can't say that I've heard of it. Can you describe it?"

"It has big membrane-like wings, with beady eyes, and its body is round and short… as in not as tall as me. And it's chubby." I pause for a moment, thinking. "And its face is ugly, and it has claws big enough to hold dragon eggs."

One of her eyebrows arches. "How many times have you seen this creature?"

"It's only been a few times, but I believe there's only one, and it's living in Asgard."

She rests a finger across her lips, and the loose ends of her pale-pink sleeve flops to her elbow. Her brow furrows into a frown. After a moment, she raises her finger. "Ah! I think I might know the one. Come, follow me." The material of her navy culottes swishes as she walks to the far wall at the back of the library. Jannika grabs the ladder and drags it to the far end of the library.

"Wait here. I shall bring it back down." She climbs and climbs, and I wonder if she is ever going to stop. Balancing on the top rung, she reaches into the shelves and pulls out a large book. Briefly, she studies the cover before tucking it under her arm and climbing down the ladder.

Her black heels land softly on the carpet, and she dusts off the cover. "It's strange, you know. It was only yesterday that someone else borrowed this for the day." She hands it to me with the cover facing up.

With both hands, I take it from her and stare at the cover. "Is this for real?"

She looks at the book and looks back at me. "Why yes, of course. Have a good look through and see if you can find the creature."

I turn to leave. "Thank you," I say at the last second, remembering my manners. She has always been kind to me. I take it to the nearest desk and start turning the pages. An artist's illustrations of strange creatures of all shapes and sizes cover the pages. After several pages, my eyes land on the exact image of the creature that marked my arm. I stare at it in disbelief and blink, trying to decide if I'm imagining things. I know I briefly saw it when the other Valkyrie had the book in the dining hall, but it is still hard to comprehend. I shove my hand in the page's position and close the book to stare at the cover. I reopen the book to the page and stare at the creature. My brain is having a hard time processing the information. Every picture in the book is hand drawn, but the likeness is still staggering.

I flick through a few more pages and find a picture of the old woman I met in the wilderness then encountered in the bathroom that day. And then I close the book again, with my arm marking my place, staring at the cover in disbelief. I open the book back to the same position then browse through a few more pages. My jaw drops. Before me, perfectly captured by the artist, is the young Valkyrie who sat at our table in the dining hall, reading this very book. To be certain, I flick back to the cover and reread it. The book is titled *Known Shapes of the Shapeshifter Loki*.

The End

ACKNOWLEDGMENTS

I am touched by the enormous amount of support I have received from my immediate family. My husband has been a helpful first reader and at times been a wonderful motivator, with hints of ideas to help me through the blanks. The support from my three sons has also been overwhelming. They have put up with my head being in the clouds, thinking about the next plot twist or story for several years. Along with many hours spent working on my books and keeping in touch with my readers.

A big thank you to my extended family who support me being a book enthusiast.

A huge thank you to my editor, Stefanie B, her editing and writing tips, and my Proofreader, Irene S, for picking up the things we missed.

Thank you to all of my readers who have loved my work, and continue to read my stories. I would love for you to share your thoughts in a review on one or all of the following:

Amazon.com
Goodreads
Barnes & Noble
You can follow Katrina Cope at:

https://www.facebook.com/Author.Katrina.Cope

https://twitter.com/Katrina_R_Cope

https://www.goodreads.com/author/show/7265107.Katrina_Cope

https://www.katrinacopebooks.com

http://http://www.amazon.com/Katrina-Cope/e/B00F00JF9M/

Book 5 of Valkyrie Academy Dragon Alliance Series 'Empowered' released October 2019.

BOOKS BY KATRINA COPE

~~~~~

Pre-Teen Books

THE SANCTUM SERIES

JAYDEN'S CYBERMOUNTAIN

SCARLET'S ESCAPE

TAYLOR'S PLIGHT

ERIC & THE BLACK AXES

ADRIANNA'S SURGE

~~~~~

Young Adult Urban Fantasy

AFTERLIFE SERIES

FLEDGLING

THE TAKING

ANGELIC RETRIBUTION

DIVIDED PATHS

Afterlife Novelette

THE GATEKEEPER

~~~~~

Young Adult Urban Paranormal Fantasy

SUPERNATURAL EVOLVEMENT SERIES

(Associated with the Afterlife Series)

WITCH'S LEGACY (#0.5 Prequel)

AALIYAH

~~~~~

Young Adult Fantasy Nordic Myths

VALKYRIE ACADEMY DRAGON ALLIANCE

SERIES

MARKED (Prequel)

CHOSEN

VANISHED

SCORNED

INFLICTED

EMPOWERED

AMBUSHED

WARNED

ABDUCTED

BESIEGED

DECEIVED

GET UPDATES & NOTIFICATIONS OF GIVEAWAYS

Would you like a FREE copy of Marked?
Visit here:
https://www.katrinacopebooks.com/valkyrie-academy-dragon-alliance
Through this link you can sign up for my newsletter and receive a FREE copy of Marked plus updates about my fantasy books, sales and notification of giveaways.

DID YOU ENJOY THIS BOOK?
YOU CAN MAKE A BIG DIFFERENCE.

Honest reviews of my books help bring them to the attention of other readers.

If you've enjoyed this book, I'd be grateful if you could spend a few minutes leaving a review (it can be as short as you like).
The review can be left on Amazon and Goodreads.
Thank you very much.

ABOUT THE AUTHOR

Katrina is an author of several Young Adult and Preteen/Middle Grade novels. Each of her released books reaching the top 100 in certain categories on the Amazon's Best Sellers Rank – a few even as high as number one.

She resides in Queensland, Australia. Her three teenage boys and husband for over nineteen years treat her like a princess. Unfortunately though, this princess still has to do domestic chores.

From a very young age, she has been a very creative person and has spent many years travelling the world and observing many different personalities and cultures. Her favourite personalities have been the strange ones, yet the ones under the radar also hold a place in her heart.

During her last extensive travels, she spent 16 nights in a bomb shelter on a Kibbutz 8 kilometers off the Lebanese border. It was to avoid Katyusha bombs that the resident volunteers decided to name her after (she is still trying to work out why).

Katrina's online home is at www.katrinacopebooks.com

You can connect with Katrina on:

Twitter https://twitter.com/Katrina_R_Cope

Facebook
https://www.facebook.com/Author.Katrina.Cope

Instagram
https://www.instagram.com/katrina_cope_author

Pinterest
https://www.pinterest.com.au/katrinacope56

Email authorkatrinacope@gmail.com